Jemmy Button

FOR NOAH, MY HOME—J. U.
TO MY GRANDPARENTS—V. V.

First U.S. edition 2013

Library of Congress Catalog Card Number 2012942662
ISBN 978-0-7636-6487-9

12 13 14 15 16 17 TLF 10 9 8 7 6 5 4 3 2 1

Printed in Dongguan, Guangdong, China

This book was typeset in Gill Sans and Strangelove Text.
The illustrations were done in gouache, oil paintings, and collage.

TEMPLAR BOOKS

an imprint of
Candlewick Press
99 Dover Street
Somerville, Massachusetts 02144
www.candlewick.com

JENNIFER UMAN & VALERIO VIDALI

Jemmy Button

WORDS BY ALIX BARZELAY

templar publishing

Once, long ago, on a faraway island, there was a boy.

Some nights he climbed to the tallest branch of the tallest tree
to look at the stars. He listened to the lap of the waves and wondered
what was on the other side of the ocean.

One day a boat came
with visitors.

They invited the boy to visit their land,
far away across the sea.

"Come away with us and taste our language,
see the lights of our world."

One of the visitors opened his hand to reveal a button made from the ocean's most magnificent pearl. They gave it to the boy's family. "We will call you Jemmy Button," the visitors said. Even the wind seemed to whisper, "Jemmy Button, Jemmy Button."

Jemmy Button said farewell to the island, to its trees and their boughs, and to its night sky filled with stars.

The voyage was long, across the dark, choppy sea.

On the other side of the ocean, Jemmy Button was surprised to find that the homes were made mostly of rocks, some stacked in towers taller than the tallest tree in the forest.

And there were so many people. . . .

The colors and noises and costumes made
Jemmy Button feel very small indeed.

Soon, he owned a hat and
was draped in rich fabrics.

He looked almost like everyone else.

Almost, but not quite.

Jemmy was taken
to places where
there were lights
brighter than the sun . . .

and to stages
where music was
as infinite as the ocean.

There was a king and queen
more decorated than the
wildest orchid.

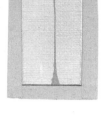

Jemmy felt almost at home.

handmade · crem

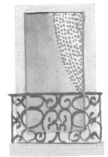

Almost, but not quite.

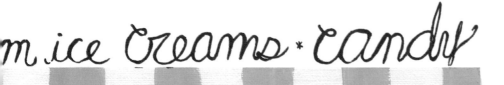

Sometimes he missed the island.
He missed the trees and their boughs,
and the stars in the night sky.
The time came to return home.

The visitors agreed he should go back and teach his people what he had learned.

All the friends that Jemmy Button had made came to see him off.

"Good-bye, Jemmy Button!" they called out.

The voyage was long, across the dark, choppy sea.

The island had remained the same, as had the forest and the sky
and the ocean.

Then Jemmy Button climbed to the tallest branch of the tallest tree and listened to the lap of the waves. He smelled the wind and heard the hush of the breeze through the branches.

"My name is Orundellico, and I have come home."

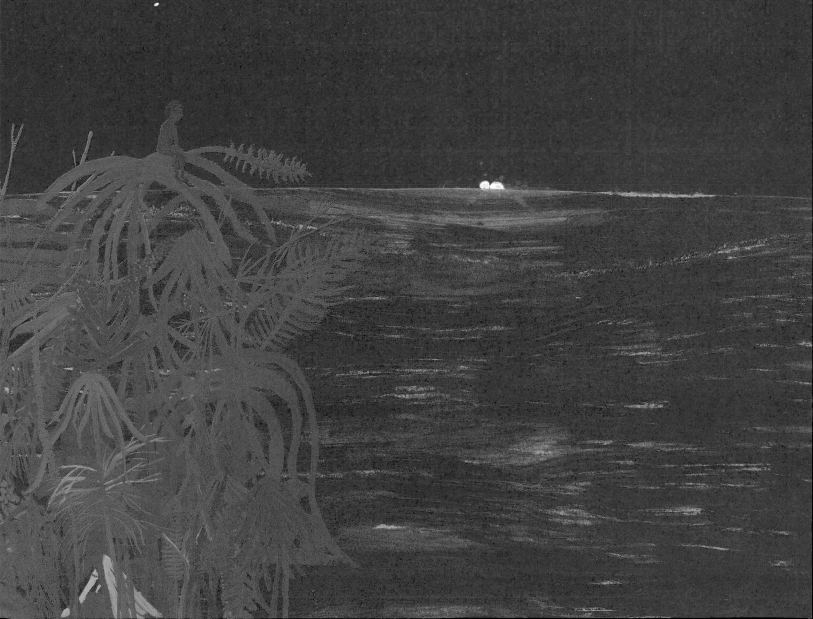

In the early 1800s, Captain Robert FitzRoy set sail on HMS *Beagle* from England to the islands of Tierra del Fuego, at the tip of South America. The captain carefully observed the indigenous people living there. He took a boy named Orundellico back to England to educate him in the ways of Christianity and Victorian upper-class customs. FitzRoy had given Orundellico's family a mother-of-pearl button in exchange for taking him, and this gave rise to Orundellico's new name, Jemmy Button. While in England, Jemmy became something of a celebrity and even attracted the attention of King William IV and Queen Adelaide.

In 1832, Captain FitzRoy returned Jemmy Button to Tierra del Fuego with the hope that he would share his acquired Victorian cultural influence among his own people. Charles Darwin, a young naturalist, joined FitzRoy and his crew on this journey. As the ship approached the shore, Jemmy realized he was home and immediately shed his clothing. With great effort, he relearned his native language, and at that point he understood where he belonged.

This book is inspired by the stories of Jemmy Button.